PRAISE FOR M

One of our favorite authors.

— RT BOOK REVIEWS

Buchman has catapulted his way to the top tier of my favorite authors.

— FRESH FICTION

A favorite author of mine. I'll read anything that carries his name, no questions asked. Meet your new favorite author!

— THE SASSY BOOKSTER, FLASH OF FIRE

M.L. Buchman is guaranteed to get me lost in a good story.

— THE READING CAFE, WAY OF THE
WARRIOR: NSDQ

I love Buchman's writing. His vivid descriptions bring everything to life in an unforgettable way.

— PURE JONEL, HOT POINT

FLYING BEYOND THE BAR

US COAST GUARD ROMANCE STORY

M. L. BUCHMAN

Buchman Bookworks

Other works by M. L. Buchman:

Short Story Series by M. L. Buchman:

The Night Stalkers
The Night Stalkers
The Night Stalkers 5E
The Night Stalkers CSAR
The Night Stalkers Wedding Stories

Firehawks
The Firehawks Lookouts
The Firehawks Hotshots
The Firebirds

Delta Force
Delta Force Short Stories

US Coast Guard
US Coast Guard

White House Protection Force
White House Protection Force Short Stories

Where Dreams
Where Dreams Short Stories

Eagle Cove
Eagle Cove Short Story

Henderson's Ranch
Henderson's Ranch Short Stories

Dead Chef Thrillers
Dead Chef Short Stories

Deities Anonymous
Deities Anonymouse Short Stories

SF/F Titles
The Future Night Stalkers
Single Titles

CHAPTER 1

*T*he beat of the Dolphin's rotors pounded into his body and Harvey Whitman did his best to tamp down the automatic adrenaline charge. The orange US Coast Guard HH-65C "Dolphin" search-and-rescue helicopter was hustling due west out of Astoria, Oregon and straight into the darkness of a Pacific Ocean nighttime gale. Blowing forty knots was so normal out here for a chill February night that the pilots hadn't even remarked on it as they'd loaded up. Something about the wild smell, the taste of the salt spray that a good storm kicked up into the air, always charged him up.

"Sea state is very rough," Vivian called out from her position as crew chief close behind the pilots but facing backwards into the cargo bay. A single strand of her dark curly hair had escaped the neatly formed bun to show between the lower edge of her flight helmet and the upper edge of the international orange survival suit they all wore. He'd always liked that curl. Even back before he knew Vivian Schroder's name, it had captured his

1

attention. Not that the rest of her didn't, but there was something special about that renegade lock on the otherwise perfectly squared-away petty officer.

"Like that's news," Harvey didn't need to be able to see the nighttime ocean to know that. A Douglas Sea Scale State of 6, or "very rough" meant six-meter waves. Two-story high, wind-shredded surf rated as a typical dose of ugly for this stretch of the Pacific. "Just another day at the beach."

Vivian laughed over the intercom. Something she'd done every time he spoke his dad's ritual phrase.

"Just another day at the beach," Harvey recollected. *Sure, Dad. Except you were a Navy clerk for two years in San Diego and never spent a day on the water no matter how many tales you'd spun for all those years—before I figured out how to look up your service record.* Actually, confronting his father hadn't changed a thing: Dad's stories or his complete lack of interest in his son.

"Ten minutes," one of the pilots called back.

As the helo jounced through the storm, Harvey was glad to be doing the prescribed routine tasks. Thinking about his dad was never a good sign. He started prepping in case he had to go into the water. He double-checked the ankle, wrist, and neck seals on his wet suit. He'd already pulled the long beaver-tail of his jacket between his legs and attached it to the front of his jacket. Tapping the closures of his harness assured him that everything was in place. A habit-trained series of slaps located: radio, flashlight, knife, hammer for shattering glass with a hook for cutting straps, diver's knife, and magnesium flare. All in place.

He could see Vivian's eyes following the same pattern as she visually confirmed everything he touched.

"Anything new?" He knew that they would have told him if there was. That he would have heard the call coming in over the intercom. It didn't stop his need to know what he was getting into. Despite the drama in the movies, rescue swimmers didn't enter the water all that often and he wondered if tonight would be one of the exceptions.

"Nothing new," Vivian offered a lopsided smile at his need to know. Her smirk was almost as much of a tease as the stray curl of hair. "Fishing charter *Albatross*. It's a Bayliner 35."

He groaned to fill the pause she'd left for him to do just that. They all knew that Bayliners were designed to look good sitting at the dock. Smooth-water boats, they were never meant to go for deep-water halibut fifty miles offshore in February. Most of the Coast Guard's rescues were in the turbulent waters of the Columbia River Bar or hunting for people dragged out to sea by the coast's vicious rip tides. Where the river hit the Pacific was rated as the most dangerous shipping waters in the world and called for frequent assists within easy reach of the Guard's forty-seven-foot motor lifeboats. Not tonight.

"Six aboard." Which would load up the Dolphin to its capacity: the four crew aboard now plus the six rescued from the Bayliner. It was going to get tight in here fast. And that was assuming everything went well.

Of course they might not need rescuing at all. Most of the time it was a matter of telling them they were fine. If the situation was bad, their Dolphin's flight would pinpoint the endangered boaters so that a motor lifeboat or cutter could come out and give them a can of fuel or a tow. Only if it was dire would the USCG send a rescue swimmer into the water to help airlift them out.

A Bayliner 35 in two-story waves—they were probably just all too seasick to stand up.

CHAPTER 2

"They were probably blind drunk." Vivian recalled Harvey's declaration about her parents at their first meal together two months ago.

"They probably came here first," she responded, because it was about the most unlikely circumstance on the planet. Her parents in an Astoria, Oregon bar was never going to happen. Especially not one like this.

Besides, it was Christmas Eve, always a big affair at the Adler mansion. Instead of surviving Mother's endless matchmaking, it was her third day in Oregon and Vivian had nowhere else to go. It was calm and unusually cold for the Oregon Coast—just below freezing, her breath had clouded on the night air as the whole team hustled out to Workers Tavern. It lay on a dirty back street under the Astoria-Megler Bridge that spanned the Columbia River between Oregon and Washington on the Oregon side.

The place was a total dive, and the owners were proud of that. Just in case there was any doubt, "Dive Bar" was prominently displayed in the front window below the glowing red-and-green "Breakfast All Day" sign and the blue Pabst neon. Inside was deeply marine: dark wood walls that might have been ripped off sunken ships, life rings, oars, funky art, a mounted five-foot-long fish that she didn't recognize but definitely declared "we grow them big here", more craft beer logos than you could count—though none so prominent as the big circular Buoy Beer Co. sign.

Most of one wall was covered in small currency bills from all over the world stapled to the wood. One of the pilots had inspected them carefully and declared that a third of them no longer even existed. The Australian pound, the Taiwanese yen, Israeli lira—he listed off a bunch of them. "And that's before you get into the nineteen countries now using the euro."

"The place has been a port dive bar since 1926. Get a lot of drunken sailors from a world of ports in that time." Harvey had explained for her benefit.

Vivian wished she could get drunk. But both of their crews were on call so they all had tea or coffee with their prime rib—apparently a Workers Tavern specialty. The air was thick with the smell of grilled burgers and fries from the tiny corner kitchen tucked behind the massive U-shaped bar. She, Harvey, and the six other Coasties of their two helicopter crews had taken over one of the battered tables close by the front windows.

The lead and backup crew didn't have to sit out at Air Station Astoria, but they had to be available for immediate deployment—which meant, "Don't leave town and you'd better be stone cold sober." Quite how that had turned into Christmas Eve dinner in a dive bar was something that still eluded her.

Sylvester and Hammond, her assigned pilots, had sworn this was the greatest place in all of Astoria. Having only just made it into town from the Aviation Training Center, she had nothing to judge by. The ATC, located in Mobile, Alabama, had also been far warmer. She'd wanted out of Alabama before another summer hit and had filed her request five days ago, knowing it could take months to fill. USCG thinking had figured that meant she should be posted to Oregon within the week in the dead of winter.

Astoria, Oregon? It was the sort of place that her parents had to look up on a map before properly showing their disdain, "Really, dear?" It had been their favorite phrase for dealing with their difficult daughter. Ambition was frowned upon for old Southern families. Especially the kind of ambition that had led her into the high school auto shop instead of the glee club or the cheerleading squad.

Then, to add insult to injury, instead of going to Clemson (where her sister had married a very eligible heir to a shipping empire) or the University of South Carolina (where her brother the lawyer had just proposed to a very popular US senator's daughter, practically guaranteeing his political career)—or even, God forbid, the University of Virginia (where she'd be at risk of meeting a Yankee stockbroker, but it couldn't be helped)—she'd gone straight to the Aviation Institution of Maintenance in that heathen hellhole of Las Vegas. It hadn't taken a genius to crack their code. Her parents had clearly looked up

Southern schools with the highest "Meet Your Spouse Here" rankings.

Her parents had also tried to fire Captain Heath for "corrupting their daughter" with flying lessons in the family helicopter. She'd threatened to call the media rags with photos of both of her parents' flagrant affairs—not that she actually had photos, because...*ick!* But the threat had been sufficient to save Captain Heath's job and even up his salary.

The three years getting her Aviation Maintenance Technician Helicopter and two more working maintenance for Grand Canyon Helicopters had stood her in good stead when enlisting in the USCG. ("Maybe she'll at least marry an officer.") She'd decided to follow in Captain Heath's footsteps...but hadn't counted on that path leading to a dive bar on the Oregon Coast for Christmas Eve.

She'd been trying to explain her family to Harvey, for reasons that thoroughly eluded her. She typically did her best to pretend she was an orphan.

"They were probably blind drunk," was as good an explanation as any to explain her parents. She appreciated Harvey's levity, if not the probable accuracy of the statement. As if that would forgive any of the ways they'd tried to manipulate her.

Cocktails on the verandah at five. Mother would pour. Another one or two before dinner if there were guests, and there were always guests at the Adler's. Whether at the Mt. Pleasant house overlooking the first tee at the Snee Farm Country Club near Charleston, or at the country house out on Lake Marion two hours inland (half an hour by helo), they entertained lavishly—which included wine and after-dinner brandies. Father would pontificate. They were relatively new, banker money, so they put on far more airs than any genuine old-money plantation owner with ten times the holdings. Six generations back they had a Yankee, post-Civil War-profiteer ancestor that they kept far more hidden than their affairs. Father's family had "come into" large tracts of land surrounding Charleston, gambling on the city's recovery and expansion—a bet that had paid off very handsomely.

"They offered to buy a new building for my flight school, only if the president agreed to flunk me out first," was what she'd said that prompted his response about their state of inebriation.

Harvey's easy laugh fit right in at the dive's bar where a group of graybeards at the bar were trying to put together an unharmonious cacophony that would have definitely offended Wenceslas—whether or not he was a good king. They wore matching ball caps with pictures of beer steins on the front and the words "Christmas Cheers" in red-and-green glitter. They'd definitely had their share of Christmas beers.

She tried to read what lay behind Harvey's reaction. She didn't like revealing that she came from money—if her parents had bought the school a building, it would be far from their biggest investment that year. Revealing that wasn't her first choice. Or her hundredth.

Then why did you say it, girl? And to the overconfident Coastie she'd known less than forty-eight hours.

To shock the unflappable rescue swimmer? As if she

actually *was* more than she appeared because of her family's wealth? That was her parents' game, not hers. And if that was her goal, it hadn't worked at all. Instead Harvey looked around the bar and nodded to himself before cutting back into his prime rib—which she had had to admit was amazingly good.

"Pop would have liked this place," Harvey gave her a subject change. "I spent a lot of time as a kid in a place like this."

"You grew up in a dive bar?"

"Kinda. My pop sure grew old in one," his frown said she wasn't the only one with parents best left in the past. "But it literally *was* a dive bar down in Coronado, California. I made friends with the old, Vietnam-era Navy swimmer who owned the place. Joel trained me himself off the same beaches the Navy SEALs train from."

"And you aren't a SEAL because..." The graybeards hunched at the bar were onto something that might have been "Jumpin' Jack Flash" to the tune of "Jingle Bells." Or maybe it was "Yellow Submarine." Hard to tell.

He tipped his head as if cracking his neck. As if he was deciding whether or not to tell the truth.

She sipped her decaf coffee and waited to see where the coin was going to drop. Ten bucks would get her a hundred that he'd backpedal and cover the momentary lapse of honesty with another subject change.

Then he sighed and looked her straight in the eyes. "I decided, since I couldn't save Pop's life—even from his own, self-dug hole—that I'd rather save lives than take them."

CHAPTER 3

"Three minutes to last known pos-*i*-tion," Hammond announced over the Dolphin's intercom from his left-hand command seat. There was a distinct hiccup in his voice when they slammed through an air pocket. Sylvester would be handling the bulk of the flying from the right seat.

The tightness in Harvey's neck wasn't going away. It could be three minutes to action or two hours before they had to return for a refuel if they couldn't find the lost Bayliner. Either way, they were in for a hard ride—the storm was still on the build and was slapping around the helo like a baby bird on its first flight.

"Permission to open doors?" Harvey called forward. It was never a good idea to surprise a pilot.

"Okay to open doors," Hammond acknowledged.

Harvey snapped a monkey line from his vest to a D-ring by the door and gave each end a good tug to make sure he didn't get thrown out the open cargo bay door by some nasty turbulence. Only after that did he unbuckle from the small jump seat at the rear of the cargo bay. Vivian remained belted into her seat, which could slide side-to-side so that she could work from close beside either door of the cargo bay.

What mattered now was eyes on the water. More than half the challenge of a rescue was finding the boat in the first place. The fact that there'd been no updates could mean that the Bayliner's passengers had simply forgotten to keep transmitting updates, that their radio's battery had shorted out, or that all that was left to be found was a couple of bodies kept afloat by their life preservers.

Vivian slid her seat all the way to the port side to watch out the massive window of the emergency exit door.

Harvey moved forward enough to unlatch the heavy starboard door. It edged out three inches, then slid backwards to slam into the end of its track. Before leaning out to look, he gave it a tug to make sure it had latched open and wasn't going to come sliding forward like a renegade guillotine when they hit the next air pocket.

"Gotta whole lot of nothing out this side." The pilots had the landing light shining forward, hoping to spot debris or even a smoothing of the wave surface from leaked diesel fuel. But looking off to the side, there were black clouds so thick that not even moonshine could make them glow. A hundred feet below them was the hungry maw of the Pacific waters that had eaten more than two thousand ships since Robert Gray first crossed the Bar in 1792, though Native traditions spoke of washed-up Asian and European ships all the way back to 1700.

"Oh, it's all bright and so purty out this side," Vivian announced breathlessly, actually getting him to turn and look. "Astoria looks like fairy lights at this time of night." Which was fifty miles behind them—five hundred feet would be a good visibility in this mess.

The woman had made him a sucker for a straight line. Just to rub it in, she wasn't even looking out the window as she said it, instead watching him turn and fall for her line. Yeah, she had him, hook, line, and sinker in more ways than one. He turned back to his own window to hide the smile that would have said just how much he was loving it.

Lives on the line somewhere below them, and still Vivian kept a cheerful and positive attitude. Harvey wasn't nearly as good at that as she was, yet another thing to admire about her. In the two months since she'd arrived in Astoria and they'd started flying together, it never varied. Nobody could be that consistently upbeat— yet it didn't feel like a facade.

When they'd lost that college student to stupidity on New Year's Eve. She'd gone quiet, but not downbeat.

The kid and his buddy had gone out on the beach at Seaside, Oregon to play around on an eighty-foot log at least four feet in diameter. Didn't they get that the ocean had put it there and could toss it around any time it wanted? There were plenty of signs posted to stay off the driftwood—but they'd ignored those. They hadn't even started drinking yet, so they hadn't had that as an excuse either.

The kid washed out to sea had been the lucky one, probably dead from hypothermia inside the first ten minutes. His buddy had almost bled to death before they could dig him out from where a sneaker wave had lifted the twenty-five-ton log long enough for him to fall under it before the water dropped it back down. He'd had to have both of his legs amputated. They finally found first kid's battered body washed up on boulders far out along the South Jetty of the Columbia River, ten miles to the north of Seaside.

No graveyard humor defense mechanism from Vivian. Just a soft curse as Harvey had ascended from the wave-beaten jetty on the winch with a body latched onto his harness.

She'd helped him tuck the kid into a body bag without flinching, then rested a hand on his arm. Just rested it there until he could feel the human connection through the thick neoprene swimmer's suit. Until he could get past the first time he'd ever handled a dead body in three years as a rescue swimmer. He'd lost people. Saving two off a crab boat before it sank with the other four hands already dead. But he'd never had to recover a dead person before.

He hoped there was no repeat tonight because finding that kid had been the New Year's present from hell.

CHAPTER 4

"This is getting to be a habit," Vivian couldn't believe that she was back in Workers Tavern—ever. Being here for both Christmas and now New Years was just flat out unnatural.

Mother was threatening to fly out in the family jet to visit her baby girl. Maybe she'd bring Mother here. The graybeards would go crazy over the perfectly-maintained blonde-and-seriously-built Southern belle... Mother just might like that. Vivian blessed that she had taken the darker coloring and slender build of Father's side, allowing her to blend into the background a little better.

The graybeards' Christmas hats had been changed. Instead of two frothing beer mugs with "Christmas Cheers," their hats now had an empty mug and a full one on them and "New Years = New Beers" in silver glitter. They seemed uncertain about climbing the mountain of "Auld Lang Syne" and were now either doing injustice to ABBA's "Happy New Year" or slaughtering "New Year's

Day" by Taylor Swift to the tune of Judy Garland's "Over the Rainbow."

Tonight she and Harvey were off shift. Not even in the wings as the backup crew. They'd spent five hours in the air looking for the second boy before finding his remains out at the jetty. The Senior Chief had taken one look at Harvey and told her to take him out and get him drunk.

Having only been in Astoria for ten days, Vivian had taken him to the only bar she knew.

She'd had the French Dip with French fries. He'd had the French toast with bacon and sausage, but not risen to the bait of her teasing in French—even after he'd confirmed that he spoke a high school's worth.

An hour later they were still on their first beers. So much for getting him drunk.

"Tell me something, anything." It was the first time that he'd actually spoken first since they'd hauled that body aboard. Poor drowned boy. Senior in college which made her about three years and an entire lifetime older, except now his lifetime was done.

How did life get so short?

But that didn't seem like the right opener at the moment. She didn't know what to say, so she answered his question with a question, hoping it would help him get past whatever he was feeling.

"Tell me about that Navy swimmer. Joel, was it?" And apparently, she'd hit exactly the right topic.

It rapidly became clear that the young Harvey had taken all that love that his father hadn't cared about and heaped it on the SEAL sixty years his senior. It sounded so clear in his voice it might have been the ringing of a

New Year's bell, though he spoke no louder than enough to be heard across the table in a noisy bar. The aged regulars at the bar had descended to a vague form of karaoke, singing along with whatever Golden Oldies were being performed in the televised Times Square celebration where it was almost midnight already.

"Joel didn't know the meaning of half measures," Harvey actually finished his beer and ordered another. She was driving, so she kept nursing her first one. "He took me out to Catalina Island on the ferry one evening near sunset. All we had was a wetsuit, fins, and a snorkel. As soon as we stepped onto the dock, he pushed me over the side into the water. Figured we'd be doing a little recreational swim or something. I was fourteen and pretty convinced I knew everything I'd ever need to know by that point."

"Instead?"

"Instead he jumped in beside me, just bobbing up and down for a long moment, then he pointed out of Avalon Harbor toward the mainland."

She knew that a final, long-distance night swim was part of Rescue Swimmer training. There was a reason the Coast Guard rescue swimmers were considered to be the absolute elite. Them and the Air Force PJs—no one else was better. Their training course typically had an eighty percent failure rate.

But this didn't sound like he was telling a USCG tale. He was talking about something important. Honest men not just trying to get into her pants were outside her experience, but Harvey kept being that.

"I couldn't wrap my head around what he meant.

Despite the busy harbor and all of the crowded waterfront restaurants and shops, all I can remember was the silence down there on the water at the foot of that long stone pier. It was so vast that it echoed. Joel just looked at me and said, 'Well, you just gonna tread water all night?' I thought about telling him to go to hell. Instead, I took one last look at the comfortable ferry that was still unloading, turned the other way, and started swimming. Figured I'd show him just what was what. Seventy if he was a day, he stayed right beside me the whole way. Didn't speak again for thirty-two-point-three kilometers. That's the shortest slice across the channel. We actually swam closer to forty by where we finally fetched up."

"How did you find your way?" He hadn't mentioned having a compass.

"Stars," Harvey waved a fork up toward the bar's ceiling stained black with years of smoke off the kitchen grill. "I navigated back to the mainland using the stars. The ships go every which way through that channel so they gave no clues, though we had to avoid those as well. From the height of a two-meter swell, the horizon lies less than four kilometers away. That's as far as you can see ahead even under ideal conditions—one-tenth of the distance we covered. We finally fetched up on Balboa Peninsula at Newport Beach seventeen hours later."

"*Seventeen?*" She tried to do an hour in the pool a couple times a week. To swim for seventeen straight hours in the ocean was… Vivian didn't know what it was other than amazing.

"He didn't speak once that whole time until we landed

on the beach in front of those luxury homes and lay like a pair of dead fish. Our throats were raw with sea salt and dehydration. Our faces and the backs of our hands, the only exposed places, were sunburned lobster red. The hardest part was the last five meters, hauling myself out of the water and up onto that dry beach as a crowd of gawkers gathered around us. They actually called the cops on us like we were an invading force."

"What did he say?" What could Joel have possibly said that could tell a fourteen-year-old boy just how amazing he was, despite his father?

"He said, 'Now you know what *that* feels like'."

"He *what?*" Her shout was loud enough to get all the graybeards at the bar losing what little rhythm they had as they turned to look over at her. "He didn't tell you how incredible that was or anything?"

"Nope," now Harvey was starting to smile for the first time since they'd been called out on this morning's search for the college kid washed out to sea.

"I don't get it."

"Joel gave everything he had to teach me that limits are only there as long as we believe in them. Sure, what I did was a damned tough swim."

"Duh!"

"What Joel really showed me was that even at seventy he still didn't believe in limits."

It was only after she'd taken him home and they'd made love that night—because if Harvey the boy had been incredible, the man he'd become was amazing—that he returned to the story. As New Year's Eve midnight rolled across the Pacific Time Zone, with her curled up against

Harvey and him toying with a single lock of her hair, he whispered so softly as if he was afraid the world would hear.

"He never swam again. Died less than six months later —mercifully fast, a stroke and gone. I always feel as if he passed the best of himself to me during that long night-and-day swim. After that he knew he was done."

She turned her face into his shoulder to breathe him in. He didn't smell of the ocean or even of wet neoprene that always seemed to permeate her skin for days after wearing a wetsuit.

"I keep thinking about that kid today. I'm wondering if someone had passed something on to him and now it was cut off."

"Joel gave you so much," Vivian almost felt envious. "All you can do is do your best to live up to that."

He considered, tugged lightly on the lock of her hair once more, then she could feel his nod.

As he turned to make love to her at the start of the new year as he had at the end of the old one, she knew what he smelled like. It was something she had so little experience with that it had taken her lying in his arms for hours to recognize it.

He smelled like hope.

CHAPTER 5

"Ahoy! I've got a flare," Vivian's voice sang out loud and clear over the intercom.

Harvey's eyes actually hurt from the entire hour they'd been quartering back and forth across the violent waves searching for any sign. The silence had been as echoing as that long-ago day by the Catalina Island pier. The whine of the engines, the beat of the rotor, and the howl of the wind did little to penetrate the wall of six people's lives at stake.

Now a flare. Someone had survived. The helo must have finally flown close enough for the blacked-out boat to have spotted them.

In moments, they were hovering above the pitching craft. It was still afloat, but that was about all it had going for it. The waves—now at least the three stories tall of Sea State 7—were washing it end-to-end. All semblance of "pretty" had been ripped away: canvas, seat cushions, even the plastic windshields were now little more than twisted metal frames. The survivors were huddled miserably in the cockpit. At least they were wearing life vests, but how soon before hypothermia started taking them out—if it hadn't already—he couldn't tell from up here.

"What's the nearest cutter or lifeboat?"

"An hour out."

Harvey knew exactly what that meant. That boat didn't have an hour. They'd be lucky if it had fifteen minutes. "How much time do we have left?"

"Bingo fuel in twenty-seven minutes," Hammond called back. "Fighting the storm really is chewing it up."

"Let's get the basket moving! Diver off headset." Harvey didn't wait for the response before peeling off his headset and pulling on his swimmer's hood, googles, and snorkel. Once he had those secure, he began on his fins. He turned to shout at Vivian that they needed to deploy the lift basket *now,* but she already had it unfolded and was just waiting for him to get out of the doorway.

Perching on the edge, with his feet dangling out over the deep, he waited for her.

She slid her chair close behind him and locked it in place.

When her hand rested on his shoulder, the whole situation snapped into sharp focus. For six weeks since she'd first touched his arm after that failed New Year's rescue, the merest contact with her did that to him. Whether it was on a mission, walking down the street holding hands, or curled up in bed together didn't matter.

Right now, he could see the rise and slap of the waves. The way every fifth one slammed through with an extra ferocity. The sluggish wallow of the down-flooded hull.

The debris field of canvas and lines dragging off the stern. All that crap served to make a sea anchor that kept the boat's bow pointed mostly into the waves—that's what had saved them. But it would be a death trap to a diver.

"Boat or water drop?" Vivian shouted. She didn't need to ask if he was going in. Any rescue was at the swimmer's discretion, but as long as there was a soul breathing down there, she knew he was going.

He was about to call for her to winch him down onto the boat when a wave slapped sideways across the boat and nearly tumbled it.

"Water."

"Definitely. We'll drop you upwind."

Harvey set his goggles and allowed himself to feel nothing but her hand on his shoulder. Listen to nothing except the quiet words they shared only in the deepest darkness of the night. Those moments together which oddly felt like when he'd been hanging with Joel. Vivian's arms were the place he was *supposed* to be.

The Dolphin had exceptional visibility for the pilots, but the final call was up to the crew chief, because only she could see directly below and even behind.

"Continue at four o'clock." They eased over and finally passed the boat. "Give me a nudge dead astern." She placed him exactly upwind.

He was just about to point out that he didn't want to be swept into the side of the boat by the very first wave that slapped him, but there was no need. Vivian continued her adjustments until she had the helo exactly where she wanted it.

She'd been doing the same to him—or perhaps they'd

been doing it to each other. Six years in the Guard and he'd never flown with someone who he could so utterly trust. Not that the other guys had been bad. Nor was it that she was a woman who consumed his waking thoughts as thoroughly as she did his body, though she did. She was simply that exceptionally good.

"Were you top of your class?" Harvey had asked her one night as they lay awake with the dawn.

"Were you?" She shot it back short and sharp. Thankfully, her issues weren't his issues and he'd long since learned to answer those odd parental-reaction buttons of hers by remaining dead calm. It let her catch herself and cool down rather than heating up even more.

" 'A' School doesn't quite work like that," he'd answered her. "To graduate as an Aviation Survival Technician is half a year of learning to survive. If you survive, you're sent to a two-month EMT course and a six-month internship. Yeah, I could outswim the other guys, but that's about ten percent of being a Rescue Swimmer."

"Oh," she sounded deeply chagrined. Then she buried her face against his shoulder and he'd indulged himself in toying with her softly curling hair. She continued, "Getting to crew chief is a little different. Yes, I was top of my class and we were *insanely* competitive with each other." She said it like she was waiting for some judgement of why hadn't she somehow done better. She'd mentioned that the reverse putdown was also really popular in her family: "Oh, I guess the other people in your class aren't very good."

"Thought so," was all he said.

"Why?" she eventually whispered into his pectoral muscle.

"Because you're the best crew chief I've ever flown with."

"The best what?" She'd scooted up enough to take his earlobe in her teeth—hard.

"Flying with you is awesome," he held out.

"*And?*" She growled through clenched teeth.

"Oh yeah. I like your body, too."

"Harvey Whitman! You're—"

He'd never found out what he was, because he'd set about showing her exactly what he thought of her body and the wonderful things it could do to him.

"Swimmer ready?" She shouted over the roar of the rotors, bringing him back to the present.

He gave her a thumbs up.

"Deploying swimmer!" She held his shoulder hard for just a moment, as hard as when the releases shot through her shuddering body, then she slapped his shoulder and he pushed out of the helo.

Her timing was perfect, as always. The helo was hovering two stories above the wave tops, which was five stories above the troughs. A five-story fall into the sea would hurt like hell, ten stories would likely kill him. A two-story drop barely gave him time to grab his goggles with one hand so they weren't ripped off when he hit the water and wrap the other arm across his chest to keep his extra gear pinned in place.

The cold water was a hard slap anyway, but he was too

pumped up to notice more than that. He surfaced with his raised thumb breaking the water first. By the time his head broke the surface, he slammed that raised arm into the water and speed-crawled down the wave face toward the boat. It took two minutes swimming flat out to reach it, despite body-surfing down the wave faces.

He hit the side of the boat, literally, but managed to grab the chrome bow rail one-handed. He yelled out against the wrenching pull as the boat lifted its nose high off the wave. If he let go, the bow could crash down on his head and the Coast Guard would need a new rescue swimmer.

Harvey hung on until the bow slammed down over the back of the wave. He let himself float up and executed a back flip over the rail and onto the deck as the boat buried its bow underwater.

On the next climb out of the water, he let the runoff sweep him along the deck until he reached the cockpit. There he slid sideways into the seating area and crashed into one of the people huddled there. Pretty clean entry.

"Hi there. My name is Harvey Whitman and I'll be your Rescue Swimmer today." The rote phrase marked the move to the next phase of the operation even as it consoled the survivors. "How are we doing, folks?"

He answered the question for himself. Three shaking so badly that they'd need a hospital soon if they were going to live. Two alert. One unconscious or close enough.

"We're going to be lifting you out by basket today."

"What about my boat?" Alert Number Two shouted over the wind and the waves, identifying him as both the captain and a man without a clue. Portly was too kind a word to describe the man's massive girth.

"Let's worry about your people first, okay?" *And your boat is going to the bottom of the ocean any minute; you're an idiot if you don't already know that.*

CHAPTER 6

*V*ivian never tired of watching Harvey work. The world simply moved more smoothly around him. Even as he appeared to be calming someone, he casually raised an arm to signal for her to lower the basket, pointing to the downwind side of the boat.

She already had it hooked to the winch on the pylon just outside the cargo bay door. As the basket lowered, she kept a gloved hand on the wire. Part of it was so that she could feel any frays to the cable. It also let her dampen oscillations of the swinging basket and feel what the world's wind was doing, because it was hard to tell up here under the main rotor's downwash.

A wave slapped the basket, threatening to drive it into the group of survivors despite her lowering it on the downwind side of the boat.

Harvey grabbed it and wrestled it into place. All those miles he did in the pool every morning did far more than give him a magnificent body for her personal pleasure. It

made him appear effortless in situations that mere
mortals would be lucky to survive.

He'd taught her that so many times since they'd met.
Not that he was exceptional—that was a given—but that
she was. At first she hadn't believed him. But there was
only so many times you could hear something and refuse
to believe it.

That's what her parents, her family had done. For her
entire life up until this last Christmas, she'd always been
"less than." Harvey saw her as "more than." And he said it
so often, that she'd come to believe it as well—almost.

Vivian could see that there was an argument down on
the deck, which Harvey solved by bodily lifting someone
into the basket, then spinning his arm over his head. For
the moment he was touching the basket, she'd swear she
could feel him right up the wire clenched in her hand.

As she reversed the winch to lift the basket and the
first rescuee, she called to the pilots for a five-meter
climb. The Dolphin had a four-axis autopilot that let the
pilots set a hover and then spend their time paying
attention to everything from remaining fuel to flying
debris and rogue waves rather than fighting the controls.
Bumping up the hover altitude during the basket lift
added work for them, but it also got the survivor clear of
the boat and the next wave faster.

The winch lifted the basket to be even with the door,
but the survivor was a dead weight. She timed an air gust
that robbed the helicopter of some lift and gave a yank
just as the person went partly weightless. They tumbled to
the cargo deck like an empty sack. All she could do at the

moment was snap a safety line on the person and send the basket back down.

With every cycle of the basket down to the wallowing boat and back, each victim's condition became less acute —Harvey was sending up the worst first, exactly as he should. Frankly it was amazing any of them were alive with how little appropriate gear they wore. The Pacific Northwest winter called for wetsuits and Mustang float jackets, not a sweater and a slicker. The fourth one managed a muttered "Thanks" but was still shaking too hard to even crack her own heat pack. Vivian cracked one for her and tucked it in the front of her jacket. Warming up their extremities was too great a risk. She had to heat their cores first or risk making their maxed-out hearts fail.

On the fifth lift, Harvey nearly had to wrestle the remaining Survivor Number Six to the deck to let the basket rise. Because of the momentary delay, a wave caught the basket—heavily weighted with Survivor Number Five—and smacked it hard into Harvey's back. It sent him sprawling before she could get it aloft.

It took all the training the Coast Guard had ever given her to keep her cry of fear inside.

CHAPTER 7

*H*arvey seriously considered throwing the boat's owner over the side and let there only be five survivors.

God damn, but his shoulder hurt. And his knee where he'd caught it as he crashed to the deck.

Whatever happened to the old adage of captain being last off? Letting the man go down with his ship sounded pretty good at the moment. Harvey had spent as much time arguing with the guy as watching the waves. Too much time.

It had taken Harvey a while to realize the guy was mostly drunk, just used to hiding it well. He'd certainly seen it on Dad enough times—the "functional" drunk. It should have made Captain Dan far more susceptible to hypothermia, but perhaps his bulk buffered him.

Foolishly, Harvey thought that the self-proclaimed captain made a good distraction from the decaying condition of the boat. The bow wasn't even lifting clear of the waves anymore.

However, being so distracted from his job that he'd let a basket clobber him absolutely wouldn't do. He lay sprawled over what had once been the captain's pride and joy, the pilot's console with twice the number of controls and readouts than the boat really needed. Sound system controls, remotely operated searchlight (which the guy probably used for illegal night fishing), auto-pilot (that definitely should have been set to never let the guy leave the harbor), and more.

He shrugged a shoulder. Big damn mistake!

He dragged his focus back to the crisis; his head swam with a bout of nausea like he hadn't had since drown-proof training back in A School. He wasn't ready for the next wave that plastered him in the face and stole his breath away.

A chance grab at the steering wheel was all that kept him aboard as the biggest wave yet swept the boat. The other hand wasn't cooperating so well.

Something tried to push him aside. Then it thudded into his gut, but the blow was slowed by the water. Still, it drove out what little air he'd managed to catch. He was about to release his hold and hope he could follow the bubbles to the surface in the dark, when he resurfaced into the storm.

Beneath him, trapped against the deck between the console and the captain's chair, was the beefy boat's owner. That's what had hit him in the gut. But the prolonged dunking seemed to have taken most of the fight out of him.

The basket almost caught Harvey again on the next swing, but he managed to grab it, and heave the sputtering captain in. He was about to latch himself onto the basket and ride up with it from the doomed boat when his head cleared enough to ask the crucial body-count question.

"You're the last one, right? There were six of you. Right?"

"Six. Sure. Except for the dead one in the cabin."

Harvey's blood chilled. Something didn't sound right. If the others had survived out here in the elements, why would the one in the cabin be dead? He let his harness drop and waved the basket aloft.

"Harve—" Vivian's voice crackled over the radio. "We're bing…el in thre…utes."

"Roger, just have to check something."

"Repe—" was all he got back. Three minutes to bingo fuel, he didn't waste time repeating his words. Besides his bad arm was coming online now. The blow that had merely hurt, now screamed like a beast each time he tried to use his right hand.

The cabin door had been shut the entire time. The chances were that it was all that was keeping the boat afloat.

Watching the waves, he waited until they were sliding down the back of one. If he was right, once he opened the hatch, he'd have only ten to fifteen seconds before the next wave or two swept the boat under for good.

The boat punched through a wave rather than climbing over it. A chaotic cross wave actually rolled the boat, but he hung on until it righted itself. After it punched through another wave without going under, there was a momentary lull.

Out of the corner of his eye, he saw that Vivian had lowered a lifting ring in place of the basket—far less likely to clobber him in the storm's growing chaos. Though he'd have to be sure to watch for the cable weight just above the hook.

He threw open the cabin door.

A truly nasty curse worthy of a severely pissed off crew chief crackled in over the radio, but it wasn't clear enough to understand so he ignored it. His radio must have taken a hit when the basket had struck him. His headlamp revealed a kitchenette on the left—with granite counters. Open cupboards revealed a pantry, well stocked with expensive alcohols. Couch to the right. Bed straight ahead in the forward point of the cabin. The water floated as high as the mattress—knee deep. No body floating in it.

He turned to exit.

Two doors that he'd rushed past on his way in.

Door Number One led to a closet.

Bank on Door Number Two.

A head—marine toilet. With someone slumped on the floor and hugging the commode, sitting in the water up to her chest.

Out of time, he slapped the woman hard on the cheek.

She coughed, sputtered, cursed. And reeked of whisky.

Alive.

Harvey grabbed her by the collar and fought her back to the deck.

She didn't wear a lifting harness, or even a life preserver.

Out of options, he snagged the lifting collar dangling from the helo's winch and shoved her arms and head through the opening. He slapped her again, brutally hard, even if it was left-handed.

"Huh? Whassup? I'm alive?" A trickle of blood ran from her lips. "Oh, wish I wasn't. My aching head."

"Stay awake and keep your arms down if you want to live. Do you understand?"

She nodded once, then again a little more convincingly.

He signaled Vivian to lift.

Nothing happened.

When his call on the radio went unanswered, he signaled more emphatically.

CHAPTER 8

*V*ivian knew what came next.

Bingo fuel wasn't something that could be argued with. Helicopters were desperately unforgiving about running out of fuel. If they didn't want to punch a hole in the ocean themselves, they had to turn for shore right now. Any arguments about reserves in the tanks were always shut down—not even up for discussion.

"Is there a cutter closer than the shore?" she begged Hammond even as she continued lifting the seventh victim.

"No. Even if there was, we couldn't land on it in this weather."

"I have six aboard, Number Seven on the line. That's capacity."

"Good. Let's go."

"Swimmer is still in the water."

"He's what? Shit! Time?" Hammond wasn't asking about time until bingo fuel, he'd called that while Harvey was still in the cabin.

"Two full minutes to unload and cycle the winch back down. Have we burned enough fuel to take the extra person?"

"We're bingo now. Average weight?" Hammond asked, his voice betraying his own anxiety through his professional cool.

Vivian surveyed the rescuees piled up like cordwood on the helo's deck. "High. Very high." There wasn't a single person aboard who could clock in at under two hundred pounds and a couple were three-plus. And even as it ripped at her, she knew what she had to do next.

Hammond held the hover for a moment longer.

Vivian kicked out the raft package. "Raft away." The container wouldn't inflate until Harvey reached it. How many rafts had auto-inflated then blown away before the engineers had learned about that one?

Over the last survivor's head, she saw Harvey diving off the boat as it planed under the water. For some reason he was swimming one-armed toward the raft.

The boat never resurfaced.

CHAPTER 9

*H*arvey sat in the Workers Tavern with his arm in a sling.

"No swimming for a month. How am I supposed to stay in shape with one damned arm?"

"How is it that you're still alive to grouse about it?" Hammond chided him but still sounded relieved.

Sylvester joined in the game, "Couldn't they have kept you in the hospital longer so that we could eat in peace?"

Vivian just looked sad. He'd told her a dozen times that he'd torn up his shoulder trying to heave the captain into the basket, because she already felt too guilty about having to leave him behind. She didn't need to know that getting clobbered by the basket had started the problem, then bodily lifting first the captain and then his wife—who her husband had left for dead—had made it so much worse.

Harvey definitely hadn't told Vivian about the bitter thirty minutes he'd spent trying to get into the raft. Once it had inflated, he could either hang onto it one-handed or get aboard, but it had taken a slow trip through Hell before Charon the mythical boatman gave him a wave that he could ride into the half-flooded raft rather than dragging him across the river Styx into Hell proper.

He did consider telling her about *why* he'd managed to hang on though.

When the captain's wife had sobered enough in the hospital to understand that her husband had abandoned her for dead, all she'd said was, "That's my Dan all over."

After the challenge of getting on the raft, Harvey then had a three-hour wait for another helo to track down the raft's emergency transponder and come fetch him. At least they hadn't had to drop another rescue swimmer into the maelstrom, he'd been able to climb into the basket himself despite the storm continuing to build and his dislocated shoulder.

Riding out a full gale gave a man a lot of time to think.

"I—Shit!" He held a fork in his non-dominant hand and stared at his slab of prime rib. This one-handed lifestyle was gonna suck big time.

"Just jab it up and eat it caveman style," Hammond suggested, then made a show of cutting a neat piece and stuffing it happily into his mouth.

"Face down in it, dog style," was Sylvester's suggestion.

Vivian thumped the butt of her steak knife on the battered table and held it there with the tip pointing straight up. "Either of you want to try sitting on it? Don't think I can't make you."

Both of the guys were officers rather than enlisted and

outranked her by at least six inches to boot. But over the last weeks, they'd learned not to argue with Vivian.

Satisfied, she made quick work of cutting her own prime rib into bite size pieces then traded plates with him.

CHAPTER 10

$\mathcal{H}$arvey stared at the plate she'd cut up until Vivian wondered what she'd done wrong.

"We both had the *same* dinner."

He nodded but didn't look up.

"Not gonna feed you when you've got a perfectly good hand."

He shook his head, that wasn't it.

She glanced sideways, but Hammond and Sylvester were chatting up a couple of local women who'd sat at the next table over. Vivian might not have much experience at being a woman in addition to being female in a very male world, but even she could see that they were selling it hard: over-bright smiles, teasing giggles, shoulders up and back to display their figures to best advantage. Couldn't the guys see that? Maybe that's what guys *wanted.* Fine, let them fall down that hole and figure their own way back out. Her problem was the rescue swimmer across the table.

"What?" She whispered low enough to not interrupt the pilots' flirtations with doom.

"It's stupid."

"If that ever stopped you, you'd have left that Captain Dan to go down with his boat and gotten on the helo."

That earned her a brief glance and an almost smile.

"Explain yourself, swimmer boy."

He slowly forked up a piece of meat and began eating. "Death is a very strange thing."

"No shit."

"No," he looked at her as directly as he always did when he was talking about something important.

Vivian was worse than a deer in the headlights when he looked at her that way. She couldn't even look down to cut the next piece of her own roast.

"We don't talk about it. Swimmers I mean. It's the enemy. We drag people from its jaws. No matter the cost," he flapped his injured arm then winced as he made his point.

"*So others may live.* That's your motto. You embody that really, really well, Harvey." And it totally scared the shit out of her even if she wouldn't have him be any other way.

The entire flight back, she'd spent every second tending the seven rescues from the Bayliner. Core heat. Dozens of cuts and bruises from the battering they'd taken—blood welling up as they warmed. Not an instant to herself.

She'd finally got the captain to shut up about suing the US Coast Guard for not saving his boat—did it by ramming an empty flare gun up under his chin and threatening to blow his head off if he said another word. She'd heard Hammond's bark of laughter over the headset after Sylvester had turned around enough to see what she was doing and then explained it to his fellow pilot over the intercom.

It was the only laugh on the flight back.

Then off-loading everyone into the line of waiting ambulances. The debriefing, the mission reports, the… madness of not being able to go back after Harvey. Their crew had hit their airborne time limit because they'd done a beach patrol flight through the stormy afternoon. The standby crew had been headed aloft even as her bird had landed. But they'd had a backup hydraulic system failure thirty miles out and had to return before reaching Harvey so that they could change birds.

She'd forced herself to remain calm in the back of the command room.

When they'd finally found Harvey. And recovered him. *And* headed for shore. Only then had she allowed herself to weep. For the first time since childhood—Mother hadn't approved of emotions other than her own—Vivian had wept. Silently, by herself in the darkness of the empty Ready Room, she'd cried herself sick.

That had been this morning. Now they were at Workers again.

Hammond and Sylvester slid over to the next table, thinking it was their charm that was working on the two local girls, not the girls seeing two Coastie officers as their tickets out of whatever their lives were like.

"Swimmers never talk about Death," Harvey continued. Death was definitely a person to him. A personified enemy to be fought to the very limits. "We try never to think about it."

"But you did? Out there in that raft?"

"But I did." Again he looked down at his plate.

"What did you figure out?" Vivian was having trouble breathing. If Harvey gave up, she didn't know what she'd do. He'd made her believe that there was a "best" in people that was worth striving for. Sure, the world had plenty of Captain Dans. But a single Harvey could offset a thousand Dans. Ten thousand.

Harvey shoved around his cut-up meat bits for a moment, studying their patterns. Or maybe studying the depths of the ocean that he'd ridden over for those long hours alone.

"No one ever made a meal for me. Just for me."

"All I did was cut up your prime rib."

"My first memories were microwave dinners and bar food."

"Get a grip, Harvey." And the first thing she was going to do was cook him a real dinner. She'd learned from one of the best private chefs in Charleston, South Carolina. She hadn't learned more than the basics, but hanging with Chef Claude had made a good escape from her parents' pre-dinner social drinking. "You were talking about Death, not quite the same as a cut-up slab of beef."

Again he raised those dark eyes. "I knew that if I gave in for even a second, the ocean would swallow me up as if I'd never been."

Vivian couldn't suppress the cold chill that ran up her spine despite the warmth of the bar.

"I also knew that even if it didn't kill me, I could never face you if I gave in for even a moment."

"Me?" She felt suddenly breathless.

"Top of the class. Best lover a man could ever ask for. And," he stabbed up a piece of meat and held it out as proof, "kindness. A guy has to do a lot to deserve that. Women like you don't exactly grow on trees, Vivian." He nodded over to pilots' table where the flirting was fast moving into far more dangerous waters than they knew.

Vivian hadn't realized that Harvey was aware of what was going on around him. But he was a rescue swimmer. Except for that one brief lapse on the Bayliner, he had intensely trained situational awareness.

"No, we women, ah…" How was she supposed to answer a compliment like that?

We're like hothouse flowers. Except that was her mother —carefully cultivated and very well-tended, perfect as long as she was in her own little world.

We're few and far between? Was she? She'd never thought of herself as special. Not before Harvey anyway.

So…what?

"You're going to pick me from the tree."

"Thought I made that clear."

"Not very. What are you talking about?"

In answer he pointed behind her. She scanned the bar over her shoulder but didn't see anything unusual.

He pointed again, directly at the four aged regulars slouched together over their beers. They were wearing hats with two faces inside a sparkly red heart. They were working their way through Queen's "Crazy Little Thing

Called Love" that was almost in the right tune—as if maybe they'd even rehearsed it a couple of times.

That's when she spotted the date on the Budweiser calendar hanging on the wall. The picture was a stout and a pilsner in a red heart. It only took her a moment longer to realize today was the fourteenth, Valentine's Day.

But there was something more going on here.

Vivian felt an odd, floating feeling. There was something familiar about the graybeards' pink hats, though she couldn't imagine what it might be. In a daze, she rose from her seat and moved up to the bar, to where she was close enough to see their hats clearly.

Close enough to see the photos of the boy and girl inside the red heart. One was her. Not some glamor shot or official photo. It was her wearing her full kit, including her helmet and grinning at the camera—grinning at Harvey who had just told her that he loved her moments before a standard patrol flight two weeks ago. It had been one of the best moments of her life.

The other photo was Harvey plunging out of a helicopter: etched against the blue sky in his black fins and International Orange neoprene, going in to battle Death man-to-man. Someone on a sailboat had snapped the photo as Harvey had jumped in to airlift a heart attack victim to shore. The head-on shot was a powerful statement of "Help is on its way."

On the graybeards' hats, there was a small set of wings below the hearts. They spread wide from a circular center which contained crossed swimming fins—the Rescue Swimmer emblem.

The old guys were grinning wildly at her as their

harmony swayed and clashed more violently than a storm-tossed sea.

A moment later Harvey's good arm slid around her waist from behind and pulled her tight back against his sling and chest.

"You're having them propose to me—for you?"

"Pretty romantic, huh?" Harvey laughed softly. "That's what I decided out there facing Death."

"What exactly?"

"So that *we* may live," he whispered in her ear as he reached up to tug on that one curl of hair he always toyed with.

He wouldn't be getting any argument from her.

OFF THE LEASH

IF YOU ENJOYED THIS, YOU'LL LOVE THE
WHITE HOUSE PROTECTION FORCE
SERIES

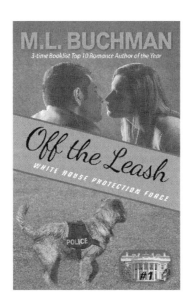

"You're joking."

"Nope. That's his name. And he's yours now."

Sergeant Linda Hamlin wondered quite what it would take to wipe that smile off Lieutenant Jurgen's face. A 120mm round from an M1A1 Abrams Main Battle Tank came to mind.

The kennel master of the US Secret Service's Canine Team was clearly a misogynistic jerk from the top of his polished head to the bottoms of his equally polished boots. She wondered if the shoelaces were polished as well.

Then she looked over at the poor dog sitting hopefully on the concrete kennel floor. His stall had a dog bed three times his size and a water bowl deep enough for him to bathe in. No toys, because toys always came from the handler as a reward. He offered her a sad sigh and a liquid doggy gaze. The kennel even smelled wrong, more of sanitizer than dog. The walls seemed to echo with each bark down the long line of kennels housing the candidate hopefuls for the next addition to the Secret Service's team.

Thor—really?—was a brindle-colored mutt, part who-knew and part no-one-cared. He looked like a cross between an oversized, long-haired schnauzer and a dust mop that someone had spilled dark gray paint on. After mixing in streaks of tawny brown, they'd left one white paw just to make him all the more laughable.

And of course Lieutenant Jerk Jurgen would assign Thor to the first woman on the USSS K-9 team.

Unable to resist, she leaned over far enough to scruff the dog's ears. He was the physical opposite of the sleek and powerful Malinois MWDs—military war dogs—that she'd been handling for the 75th Rangers for the last five years. They twitched with eagerness and nerves. A good MWD was seventy pounds of pure drive—every damn second of the day. If the mild-mannered Thor weighed thirty pounds, she'd be surprised. And he looked like a little girl's best friend who should have a pink bow on his collar.

Jurgen was clearly ex-Marine and would have no respect for the Army. Of course, having been in the Army's Special Operations Forces, she knew better than to respect a Marine.

"We won't let any old swabbie bother us, will we?"

Jurgen snarled—definitely Marine Corps. Swabbie was slang for a Navy sailor and a Marine always took offense at being lumped in with them no matter how much they belonged. Of course the swabbies took offense at having the Marines lumped with *them.* Too bad there weren't any

Navy around so that she could get two for the price of one. Jurgen wouldn't be her boss, so appeasing him wasn't high on her to-do list.

At least she wouldn't need any of the protective bite gear working with Thor. With his stature, he was an explosives detection dog without also being an attack one.

"Where was he trained?" She stood back up to face the beast.

"Private outfit in Montana—some place called Henderson's Ranch. Didn't make their MWD program," his scoff said exactly what he thought the likelihood of any dog outfit in Montana being worthwhile. "They wanted us to try the little runt out."

She'd never heard of a training program in Montana. MWDs all came out of Lackland Air Force Base training. The Secret Service mostly trained their own and they all came from Vohne Liche Kennels in Indiana. Unless… Special Operations Forces dogs were trained by private contractors. She'd worked beside a Delta Force dog for a single month—he'd been incredible.

"Is he trained in English or German?" Most American MWDs were trained in German so that there was no confusion in case a command word happened to be part of a spoken sentence. It also made it harder for any random person on the battlefield to shout something that would confuse the dog.

"German according to his paperwork, but he won't listen to me much in either language."

Might as well give the diminutive Thor a few basic tests. A snap of her fingers and a slap on her thigh had the dog dropping into a smart "heel" position. No need to call out *Fuss—by my foot.*

"Pass auf!" Guard! She made a pistol with her thumb and forefinger and aimed it at Jurgen as she grabbed her forearm with her other hand—the military hand sign for enemy.

The little dog snarled at Jurgen sharply enough to have him backing out of the kennel. "Goddamn it!"

"Ruhig." Quiet. Thor maintained his fierce posture but dropped the snarl.

"Gute Hund." Good dog, Linda countered the command.

Thor looked up at her and wagged his tail happily. She tossed him a doggie treat, which he caught midair and crunched happily.

She didn't bother looking up at Jurgen as she knelt once more to check over the little dog. His scruffy fur was so soft that it tickled. Good strength in the jaw, enough to show he'd had bite training despite his size—perfect if she ever needed to take down a three-foot-tall terrorist. Legs said he was a jumper.

"Take your time, Hamlin. I've got nothing else to do with the rest of my goddamn day except babysit you and this mutt."

"Is the course set?"

"Sure. Take him out," Jurgen's snarl sounded almost as nasty as Thor's before he stalked off.

She stood and slapped a hand on her opposite shoulder.

Thor sprang aloft as if he was attached to springs and she caught him easily. He'd cleared well over double his own height. Definitely trained…and far easier to catch than seventy pounds of hyperactive Malinois.

She plopped him back down on the ground. On lead or off? She'd give him the benefit of the doubt and try off first to see what happened.

Linda zipped up her brand-new USSS jacket against the cold and led the way out of the kennel into the hard sunlight of the January morning. Snow had brushed the higher hills around the USSS James J. Rowley Training Center—which this close to Washington, DC, wasn't saying much—but was melting quickly. Scents wouldn't carry as well on the cool air, making it more of a challenge for Thor to locate the explosives. She didn't know where they were either. The course was a test for handler as well as dog.

Jurgen would be up in the observer turret looking for any excuse to mark down his newest team. Perhaps teasing him about being just a Marine hadn't been her best tactical choice. She sighed. At least she was consistent —she'd always been good at finding ways to piss people off before she could stop herself and consider the wisdom of doing so.

This test was the culmination of a crazy three months, so she'd forgive herself this time—something she also wasn't very good at.

In October she'd been out of the Army and unsure what to do next. Tucked in the packet with her DD 214 honorable discharge form had been a flyer on career opportunities with the US Secret Service dog team: *Be all your dog can be!* No one else being released from Fort

Benning that day had received any kind of a job flyer at all that she'd seen, so she kept quiet about it.

She had to pass through DC on her way back to Vermont—her parent's place. Burlington would work for, honestly, not very long at all, but she lacked anywhere else to go after a decade of service. So, she'd stopped off in DC to see what was up with that job flyer. Five interviews and three months to complete a standard six-month training course later—which was mostly a cakewalk after fighting with the US Rangers—she was on-board and this chill January day was her first chance with a dog. First chance to prove that she still had it. First chance to prove that she hadn't made a mistake in deciding that she'd seen enough bloodshed and war zones for one lifetime and leaving the Army.

The Start Here sign made it obvious where to begin, but she didn't dare hesitate to take in her surroundings past a quick glimpse. Jurgen's score would count a great deal toward where she and Thor were assigned in the future. Mostly likely on some field prep team, clearing the way for presidential visits.

As usual, hindsight informed her that harassing the lieutenant hadn't been an optimal strategy. A hindsight that had served her equally poorly with regular Army commanders before she'd finally hooked up with the Rangers—kowtowing to officers had never been one of her strengths.

Thankfully, the Special Operations Forces hadn't given a damn about anything except performance and *that* she could always deliver, since the day she'd been named the team captain for both soccer and volleyball. She was never popular, but both teams had made all-state her last two years in school.

The canine training course at James J. Rowley was a two-acre lot. A hard-packed path of tramped-down dirt led through the brown grass. It followed a predictable pattern from the gate to a junker car, over to tool shed, then a truck, and so on into a compressed version of an intersection in a small town. Beyond it ran an urban street of gray clapboard two- and three-story buildings and an eight-story office tower, all without windows. Clearly a playground for Secret Service training teams.

Her target was the town, so she blocked the city street out of her mind. Focus on the problem: two roads, twenty storefronts, six houses, vehicles, pedestrians.

It might look normal…normalish with its missing windows and no movement. It would be anything but. Stocked with fake IEDs, a bombmaker's stash, suicide cars, weapons caches, and dozens of other traps, all waiting for her and Thor to find. He had to be sensitive to hundreds of scents and it was her job to guide him so that he didn't miss the opportunity to find and evaluate each one.

There would be easy scents, from fertilizer and diesel fuel used so destructively in the 1995 Oklahoma City bombing, to almost as obvious TNT to the very difficult to detect C-4 plastic explosive.

Mannequins on the street carried grocery bags and briefcases. Some held fresh meat, a powerful smell demanding any dog's attention, but would count as a false lead if they went for it. On the job, an explosives detection dog wasn't supposed to care about anything except explosives. Other mannequins were wrapped in suicide vests loaded with Semtex or wearing knapsacks filled with package bombs made from Russian PVV-5A.

She spotted Jurgen stepping into a glassed-in observer turret atop the corner drugstore. Someone else was already there and watching.

She looked down once more at the ridiculous little dog and could only hope for the best.

"Thor?"

He looked up at her.

She pointed to the left, away from the beaten path.

"*Such!*" Find.

Thor sniffed left, then right. Then he headed forward quickly in the direction she pointed.

CLIVE ANDREWS SAT in the second-story window at the corner of Main and First, the only two streets in town. Downstairs was a drugstore all rigged to explode, except there were no triggers and there was barely enough explosive to blow up a candy box.

Not that he'd know, but that's what Lieutenant Jurgen had promised him.

It didn't really matter if it was rigged to blow for real, because when Miss Watson—never Ms. or Mrs.—asked for a "favor," you did it. At least he did. Actually, he had yet to meet anyone else who knew her. Not that he'd asked around. She wasn't the sort of person one talked about with strangers, or even close friends. He'd bet even if they did, it would be in whispers. That's just what she was like.

So he'd traveled across town from the White House and into Maryland on a cold winter's morning, barely past a sunrise that did nothing to warm the day. Now he sat in an unheated glass icebox and watched a new officer run a test course he didn't begin to understand.

Keep reading at fine retailers everywhere:
Off the Leash

M.L. Buchman started the first of over 60 novels, 75 short stories, and an ever-growing pile of audiobooks while flying from South Korea to ride across the Australian Outback. All part of a solo around-the-world bicycle trip (a mid-life crisis on wheels) that ultimately launched his writing career.

Booklist has selected his military and firefighter series(es) as 3-time "Top 10 Romance of the Year." NPR and Barnes & Noble have named other titles "Top 5 Romance of the Year."

He has flown and jumped out of airplanes, can single-hand a fifty-foot sailboat, and has designed and built two houses. In between writing, he also quilts. M.L. is constantly amazed at what can be done with a degree in geophysics. He also writes: contemporary romance, thrillers, and SF. More info at: www.mlbuchman.com.

Other works by M. L. Buchman:

Short Story Series by M. L. Buchman:

Printed in Great Britain
by Amazon